HANG GLIDING AND PARASAILING

by John E. Schindler

GARETH**STEVENS**

PUBLISHING

A WRC Media Company

Please visit our web site at: **www.garethstevens.com**
For a free color catalog describing Gareth Stevens Publishing's
list of high-quality books and multimedia programs,
call 1-800-542-2595 (USA) or 1-800-387-3178 (Canada).
Gareth Stevens Publishing's fax: (414) 332-3567.

Library of Congress Cataloging-in-Publication Data available upon request from publisher.
Fax (414) 336-0157 for the attention of the Publishing Records Department.

ISBN 0-8368-4540-4 (lib. bdg.)
ISBN 0-8368-4547-1 (softcover)

First published in 2005 by
Gareth Stevens Publishing
A WRC Media Company
330 West Olive Street, Suite 100
Milwaukee, WI 53212 USA

Text: John E. Schindler
Cover design and page layout: Tammy West
Series editor: Carol Ryback
Photo research: Diane Laska-Swanke

Photo credits: Cover © David B. Fleetham/SeaPics.com; pp. 5, 7, 13 © Ralph Wagner/Jump;
p. 9 Courtesy of Special Collections and Archives, Wright State University Libraries;
p. 11 Courtesy of flytandem.com; p. 15 © Stephan Persch/Jump; p. 19 © Christian Perret/Jump;
pp. 17, 21 © www.guntermarx-stockphotos.com

Printed in the United States of America

1 2 3 4 5 6 7 8 9 09 08 07 06 05

Cover: A hang glider gets a bird's eye view
off the coast of Maui in Hawaii.

TABLE OF CONTENTS

Birds Do It 4

Glide Like an Eagle 6

Winging It 8

Get the Hang of It 10

Hang Gliding Gear 12

Drag and Fly 14

What to Wear in the Air. 16

Other Ways to Fly 18

Just Hanging Around 20

More to Read and View 22

Web Sites 23

Glossary and Index 24

Words that appear in the glossary are printed in **boldface** type the first time they occur in the text.

BIRDS DO IT

Did you ever want to soar through the air like a bird? A **hang glider** can help you do that!

A hang glider is a very small flying machine without a motor. It has one large wing. A hang glider rides, or glides, on moving air.

Sometimes a hang glider glides on winds that move upward, called **updrafts**. Strong updrafts might keep a hang glider in the sky for hours.

Hang gliders take off from mountains, hills, or cliffs. In flat areas, an **ultralight** aircraft can pull a hang glider into the air. An ultralight looks like a hang glider with a motor.

Moving air helps keep a hang glider in the sky. On a clear day, a hang glider can see for many miles all around.

GLIDE LIKE AN EAGLE

How do eagles, hawks, and other large birds soar high above for hours? They glide on pockets of rising warm air called **thermals**.

You can hang glide on thermals and updrafts, too. You find thermals and updrafts when air moving over high ground causes an upward pushing force called **lift**.

To ride in a hang glider, you hang underneath the glider's wing. You steer by shifting your body weight. If you lean left, you go left. If you lean right, you go right.

The trick is to stay up as long as possible. Then you can glide like an eagle!

A hang glider shifts his or her weight to make turns while high in the sky.

WINGING IT

Hang gliding is one of the oldest forms of human flight. Orville and Wilbur Wright practiced with gliders before they built the first airplane.

In the 1960s, a man named Frank Rogallo invented the Rogallo wing. It was made of cloth and shaped like a triangle. Simple metal tubes held the wing in place. These early hang gliders broke apart easily.

The 1970s brought new and better materials for building hang gliders. Hang gliders today are safer and easy to fly. Most people can learn how to fly a hang glider in just a few hours.

The Wright Brothers practiced flying a glider like this one before they invented the airplane.

GET THE HANG OF IT

Would you like to try hang gliding? Take a **tandem** flight. That means you and an instructor go up together in one hang glider. If you like tandem hang gliding, you might want to learn to hang glide by yourself.

Most hang gliding schools want you to wait until you are at least fourteen years old to take lessons. The hang gliding instructor teaches you about the gear. She also tells you what to do in the air and how to stay safe.

You can use a small radio to talk to your instructor while you are gliding high above in your hang glider.

A tandem hang gliding ride lets you enjoy hang gliding without taking lessons.

HANG GLIDING GEAR

You need to wear a helmet when hang gliding. Always wear goggles to protect your eyes. You do not want a bug in your eye up in the air! You also need sturdy shoes or boots. Wear a **jumpsuit** over your clothes for protection.

A set of straps called a **harness** fits over your jumpsuit. The harness hooks onto the hang glider to keep you safely in place. You hang under the wing and hold onto a metal bar in front of you.

If you fly higher than 300 feet (91 meters) above the ground, always wear a **reserve parachute** in case of an emergency.

A harness hangs from the frame of the hang glider and helps keep the rider safe.

DRAG AND FLY

Some hang gliders use a car to get into the air! The car drags the hang glider by a metal rope called a cable. As the car speeds up, the hang glider rises. It is just like running with a kite to make it fly.

When the hang glider gets high enough, the rider unhooks the cable. It is time to soar like a bird! The hang glider flies freely until it glides to the ground.

Parasailing is flying above water wearing a parachute. A boat goes fast to catch wind in the parachute. As the parachute rises, the rider, or parasailor, rises with it.

Parasailing is fun on a hot day. The parasailor stays hooked to the boat.

WHAT TO WEAR IN THE AIR

Hang gliders that fly really high can get pretty cold. Riders of high-flying hang gliders wear thick clothes under their jumpsuits to stay warm.

Parasailors wear swimsuits! They also wear water safety vests. Parasailing is lots of fun on a hot day.

It is also fun to ride in a boat pulling someone who is parasailing. Everyone takes turns going up. They parasail over lakes and oceans. Parasailors like to land in warm water.

You might say that anyone who parasails comes down for a splash landing!

Parasailing is a great way to cool off on a hot day!

OTHER WAYS TO FLY

Could a go-cart ever fly? Yes — if it is a **paraglider**.

A paraglider is like a go-cart with a big fan on the back. The fan moves the go-cart forward, dragging a parachute. The parachute fills with air and lifts the paraglider into the sky. Anyone can go paragliding almost anywhere.

Some people like cold weather sports, such as skiing. They can go **paraskiing**. **Paraskiers** wear parachutes to catch the wind. The parachutes pull skiers along the snow.

Some ski resorts offer paraskiing. All it takes is a parachute, a strong wind, a pair of skis — and the nerve to try it!

JUST HANGING AROUND

Hang gliding and parasailing make you feel as if you are really flying. Birds sometimes fly near you!

When you are old enough, you can find out if hang gliding is for you. Try a tandem hang gliding flight. If you like it, sign up for lessons. Soon you will hang glide high in the sky.

Parasailing is different. You do not go very high. You do not steer. You do not even need lessons for parasailing. You just sit back and enjoy the ride.

Hang gliding, parasailing, paragliding, and paraskiing can all help make your flying dreams come true!

A hang glider catches the thermals that rise up where water meets land.

MORE TO READ AND VIEW

Books (Nonfiction) *Flight. Timeliners* (series). Chris Oxlade. (Barron's)
Flying the Wing: Hooking into Hang Gliding.
    Len Homes. (Carolinas Press)

Hang Gliding.
High Interest Books: X-Treme Outdoors (series).
    Heidi Ziegler. (Children's Press)

Hang Gliding. Funseeker (series).
    Dorothy Childers Schmitz. (Crestwood House)

Hang Gliding and Parasailing: Action Sports (series).
    Toni Will-Harris. (Capstone)

The Story of Flight. Ole Steen Hansen. (Crabtree)

DVDs and Videos *Starting Hang Gliding, Fly Like an Eagle.*
    (Adventure Productions)

Starting Paragliding. (Adventure Productions)

WEB SITES

Web sites change frequently, but the following web sites should last awhile. You can also search Google (*www.google.com*) or Yahooligans! (*www.yahooligans.com*) for more information about hang gliding. Some keywords to help your search include: *history of gliders, Kitty Hawk, hang gliding lessons, sport pilot training, thermaling, trikes, weight-shift aircraft.*

disney.go.com/games/hang/
Take a virtual hang glider flight to collect flags and win this game.

www.hanggliding.plus.com/ common_qs.html
Learn the answers to many questions about hang gliding.

hang-gliding.htm
Visit this cool site to learn how a hang glider works.

ventureflight.com/page6.htm
Check out this glossary of hang gliding terms.

GLOSSARY

You can find these words on the pages listed. Reading a word in a sentence helps you understand it even better.

hang glider — a one-winged, non-motorized flying machine big enough for one person. 4, 6, 8, 10, 12, 14, 16

harness — a set of straps that attaches objects to objects or objects to people. 12

jumpsuit — a one-piece, protective covering that fits over all of your clothes. 12, 16

lift — a force that pushes upward. 6

paraglider — a hang glider with a small motor. 18

parasailing — flying above and behind a boat using a parachute. 14, 16, 20

paraskier — someone who goes paraskiing. 18

paraskiing — skiing while a parachute pulls you along the ski slopes. 18, 20

reserve parachute — a parachute that hang glider riders wear to float to the ground in an emergency. 12

tandem — built to hold two people. 10, 20

thermals — large updrafts of air that are much warmer than the surrounding air. 6, 20

ultralight — a very tiny, motorized airplane. 4

updrafts — masses of upward moving air. 4, 6

INDEX

birds 4, 6, 20
boats 14, 16

cables 14
cars 14

goggles 12

hang gliders 4, 6, 8, 10, 12, 14, 16
hang gliding 4, 6, 8, 10, 12, 16, 20

harnesses 12
helmets 12

jumpsuits 12, 16

lessons 10, 20
lift 6

parachutes 12, 14, 18
paragliders 18
paragliding 18, 20
parasailing 14, 16, 20

paraskiers 18
paraskiing 18, 20

radios 10
reserve parachutes 12
Rogallo, Frank 8
Rogallo wing 8

safety 8, 10, 12, 16, 20
snow 18

tandem hang gliding 10, 20
thermals 6, 20
ultralights 4
updrafts 4, 6

water 14, 16, 20
Wright, Orville 8
Wright, Wilber 8